Pinocchio

PUFFIN BOOKS

Published by the Penguin Group
Penguin Books Ltd, 80 Strand, London WC2R 0RL, England
Penguin Group (USA), Inc., 375 Hudson Street, New York, New York 10014, USA
Penguin Books Australia Ltd, 250 Camberwell Road, Camberwell, Victoria 3124, Australia
Penguin Books Canada Ltd, 10 Alcorn Avenue, Toronto, Ontario, Canada M4V 3B2
Penguin Books India (P) Ltd, 11 Community Centre, Panchsheel Park, New Delhi – 110 017, India
Penguin Group (NZ), cnr Airborne and Rosedale Roads, Albany, Auckland 1310, New Zealand
Penguin Books (South Africa) (Pty) Ltd, 24 Sturdee Avenue, Rosebank 2196, South Africa

Penguin Books Ltd, Registered Offices: 80 Strand, London WC2R 0RL, England

www.penguin.com

First published 2004
1

Copyright © Disney Enterprises, Inc., 2004

Set in 15/18.2 pt Cochin
Typeset by Rowland Phototypesetting Ltd, Bury St Edmunds, Suffolk

Made and printed in England by Clays Ltd, St Ives plc

British Library Cataloguing in Publication Data
A CIP catalogue record for this book is available from the British Library

ISBN 0-141-31775-2

Pinocchio

Narinder Dhami

PUFFIN

Contents

Chapter One

It was a beautiful night. The sky was dark, and the stars shone here and there like sparkling diamonds. The moon looked down over the narrow winding streets of a sleepy old town. It was late, and there was nobody around except for a little green cricket. He was hopping down the street, peering all around him. His clothes were very shabby; he wore a battered top hat and he carried a leaky umbrella. His name was Jiminy Cricket.

The only light was in the window of a wood-carver's shop. Jiminy hopped over and peeped through the window. He could see a roaring fire, but there was no one there.

'Shame to see a nice, cheerful fire going

to waste,' Jiminy said to himself, so he crawled under the door into the house.

The wood carver, Geppetto, made all sorts of things. Jiminy was amazed to see there were fantastic clocks of all shapes, sizes and colours, as well as shelves of wooden toys and little musical boxes, all carved from wood.

But the most interesting thing was a wooden puppet sitting on a bench. The puppet was the size of a real boy, and he wore a yellow hat, red dungarees and a blue bow tie. His strings hung around him, ready to make him walk and dance when someone pulled them.

Jiminy hurried over to take a look. 'Cute little fellow!' he laughed, swinging on the strings and landing on the puppet's nose. Then he heard footsteps.

'Well now,' Geppetto murmured, hurrying down the stairs. He was followed by Figaro, his black and white cat. 'It can't be long now. Just a little more paint, and he's all finished!'

2

Jiminy ran to hide as Geppetto went over to the puppet, carrying a paint pot. Carefully the wood carver painted two eyebrows on the wooden face.

'I think he'll be all right, don't you, Figaro?' Geppetto remarked, painting a smiling mouth on the puppet.

'Now I have just the name for you,' Geppetto went on, pointing at his puppet. 'Pinocchio!'

He grabbed one of the puppet's strings. 'You like it?' And he pulled the string to make Pinocchio nod. 'That settles it! Pinocchio it is. Now, we'll try you out.'

The wood carver picked up Pinocchio from the bench. Then he set one of the musical boxes playing, and began to dance around the room with the puppet. Figaro pranced after them as they whirled round and round, while Jiminy watched with a smile on his face.

DING! A clock began to strike. Then all the clocks around the room joined in loudly.

'It's getting late,' Geppetto muttered,

picking up Figaro. 'Come on, we'll go to bed. Goodnight, Pinocchio, little funny face! Goodnight, Cleo, my little water baby,' he said to the goldfish swimming in a bowl.

Geppetto climbed into bed, and Figaro jumped on to the quilt and snuggled down.

'Look at him, Figaro,' he said. He was staring across the room at Pinocchio. 'He almost looks alive!' He sighed. 'Wouldn't it be nice if he was a real boy?'

Geppetto lay down to sleep, but then sat up again.

'Oh, Figaro, look!' Geppetto gasped, pointing up at the sky. 'A wishing star.'

The stars were still shining brightly but one was bigger and brighter and more sparkling than all the others.

'Star light, star bright,' Geppetto whispered, 'first star I see tonight. I wish I may, I wish I might, have the wish I wish tonight!'

Figaro yawned.

'Figaro, d'you know what I wished?'
Geppetto went on. 'I wished that my little
Pinocchio might be a real boy!'

Chapter Two

'Wouldn't that be nice?' Geppetto sighed, as he snuggled down under the quilt again. 'Just think, a real boy . . .' and he began to snore.

The room was quiet now except for the ticking of the clocks. Geppetto, Cleo and Figaro were fast asleep but the noise was annoying Jiminy. Then, very silently, a bright star drifted down through the sky towards the open window. It filled the room with a pure white light.

'Hey!' Jiminy gasped, shooting to his feet. 'What's going on here?'

The light changed into a beautiful fairy. She had golden hair, thin gauzy wings and she wore a glittering blue dress.

'As I live and breathe – a fairy!' Jiminy murmured.

He watched in wonder as the fairy glided over to Pinocchio.

'Good Geppetto,' the Blue Fairy said, in a sweet voice. 'You have given so much happiness to others. You deserve to have your wish come true!' She pointed her wand at Pinocchio. 'Little puppet made of pine, wake! The gift of life is thine.'

The Blue Fairy touched Pinocchio on the head with her wand, and a bright light surrounded him. The light cleared, and Pinocchio moved. He rubbed his eyes.

'Whew!' gasped Jiminy.

Pinocchio waved his hands in the air. 'I can move!' he said. 'I can talk!'

He got to his feet, but grew unsteady and fell down again with a clatter.

'Yes, Pinocchio,' the Blue Fairy smiled. 'I have given you life.'

'Why?' asked Pinocchio.

'Because tonight Geppetto wished for a

real boy,' the fairy replied. 'But to make his wish come true will be up to you. Prove yourself brave, truthful and unselfish and some day you will be a *real* boy. You must learn to choose between right and wrong,' the fairy went on. 'Your conscience will tell you.'

'What are conscience?' Pinocchio asked, looking puzzled.

'I'll tell you!' Jiminy burst out, not able to keep quiet any longer. He sailed through the air using his umbrella as a parachute. 'A conscience is that still, small voice that people won't listen to.'

'Are *you* my conscience?' Pinocchio asked.

The Blue Fairy bent over Jiminy. 'Would you like to be Pinocchio's conscience?' she asked.

Jiminy turned red. 'Well – uh –' he stammered.

The Blue Fairy laughed. 'What is your name?'

'Jiminy Cricket,' Jiminy replied, raising his hat.

8

'Kneel, Mr Cricket!' the fairy told him. She held out her wand, and touched Jiminy lightly. 'I dub you Pinocchio's conscience.' Jiminy was surrounded by a bright white light. When it cleared, he was amazed to see that he was dressed in brand-new clothes, and looked very smart.

'Arise, Sir Jiminy Cricket!' announced the fairy.

The Blue Fairy turned to Pinocchio. 'Now remember, Pinocchio, be a good boy. And always let your conscience be your guide!'

The fairy faded away into the light, as Pinocchio and Jiminy waved goodbye.

'Well, Pinoke,' said the cricket, 'maybe you and I had better have a little talk!'

'Why?' Pinocchio asked.

'You want to be a real boy, don't you?' Jiminy went on. 'Now, the world is full of temptations. They're the wrong things that seem right at the time –'

'But I'm going to do right!' Pinocchio cut in.

'And I'm gonna help you!' Jiminy

9

beamed. 'And any time you need me, just whistle.' And he whistled loudly. 'Come on, let's sing it!'

Jiminy jumped on to Pinocchio's foot. 'When you get in trouble and you don't know what to do,' the cricket sang, 'give a little whistle!'

Pinocchio joined in, and he and Jiminy danced their way around the room. They made so much noise that Geppetto and Figaro woke up.

'Who's there?' called Geppetto, in a frightened voice. It was dark, and he couldn't see anything.

'It's me!' Pinocchio called gleefully. He had tumbled over, and was lying on the floor.

'Sshh, Figaro,' Geppetto whispered, putting his finger to his lips. 'There's somebody in here!'

Meanwhile Geppetto lit the candle, his hand shaking. Then he took a big old gun from under his pillow.

'Here I am!' Pinocchio cried, and touched Figaro.

The cat yelped with fright, and jumped on Geppetto. The gun went off into the air, and set all the clocks bouncing around.

'Oh, Pinocchio!' Geppetto gasped, staring down in amazement at his wooden puppet. 'How did you get down here?'

'I fell down!' Pinocchio beamed, as Geppetto put him on the bench and brushed down his clothes.

'Oh, you are talking!' Geppetto gasped.

'Yes!' Pinocchio waved at him. 'And I can move, too!'

'I'm dreaming!' Geppetto began running round the room in a daze. 'Wake me up!'

Pinocchio nodded happily. 'Yes, the Blue Fairy came, and I got a conscience!'

Jiminy smiled proudly.

'And some day I'm going to be a real boy,' Pinocchio went on.

Geppetto grabbed him and swung him into the air. 'A real boy!' he said, his eyes shining. 'It's my wish. It's come true! Figaro, look, he's alive!'

Figaro looked suspiciously at Pinocchio,

but then he let the puppet stroke him.

'Oh, I almost forgot Cleo,' Geppetto laughed. The goldfish was swimming round her bowl, looking excited. 'She's my little water baby. Isn't she cute?'

Cleo beamed. Then she jumped up out of the water and gave Pinocchio a kiss.

'This calls for a celebration,' Geppetto went on. Swinging Pinocchio into his arms, he wound up one of the musical boxes, and it began to play tinkling music. Then the old man reached for his accordion.

'Oh, boy, a party!' Jiminy laughed, as Geppetto, Figaro and Pinocchio began to dance. Cleo joined in, too, jumping around in her glass bowl.

But soon they grew tired, and it was time to go to bed. Geppetto, Pinocchio and Figaro snuggled down under the blanket together. Jiminy took off his new shoes, and settled down, too, on a shelf.

'Now, close your eyes and go to sleep,' Geppetto yawned.

'Why?' asked Pinocchio.

'Oh, everybody has to go to sleep,' Geppetto replied drowsily. 'And besides, tomorrow you've got to go to school.'

Chapter Three

It was morning, and the bell in the village tower was ringing. The village had come alive again as people hurried out of their houses, and children played in the streets.

The door of Geppetto's house opened. Pinocchio danced outside and began jumping around with excitement as he looked at the children playing.

Geppetto watched proudly as Pinocchio skipped off along the street. 'Goodbye, Father!' Pinocchio called with a cheery wave, as he ran towards the other children.

At the same moment, a fox and a cat came strolling down the street. They both wore shabby and torn clothes, and the fox had a battered top hat on his head and a cane in his hand.

'Ah, Gideon,' Honest John, the fox, sighed. 'Listen to the merry laughter of little innocent children on their way to school!'

Gideon pulled a face, but didn't say anything. He never did. Honest John speared a cigar lying on the pavement with his cane and picked it up. Just then he spotted a poster on the wall. *The Great Stromboli – Marionette Show*, it read.

'Well, well, well,' Honest John murmured. 'Stromboli. So that old rascal's back in town, eh!'

He laughed and turned to Gideon. 'Remember the time I tied strings on you and passed you off as a puppet? We nearly put one over that old Stromboli that time!' Honest John chuckled slyly.

Pinocchio came skipping down the street, an apple in one hand and a book in the other.

Honest John stopped suddenly, his mouth falling open in surprise. 'A wooden boy!'

The fox and the cat watched Pinocchio skip off down the pavement.

'It's amazing!' Honest John gasped.

'A live puppet without strings!' He stroked his chin thoughtfully. 'A thing like that ought to be worth a fortune. Quick! We'll head him off!'

Keeping out of sight in the alleyways, Honest John and Gideon dashed after Pinocchio. 'Ah, yes, Giddy, as I was saying to the Duchess only yesterday,' Honest John boomed, seeing Pinocchio skipping towards them. He stuck out his cane, and Pinocchio tripped right over it, dropping the book and the apple.

'Oh, how clumsy of me,' said Honest John, helping the puppet to his feet. 'I'm terribly sorry.'

'I'm all right,' Pinocchio replied cheerfully, as the fox and the cat brushed him down. 'I'm going to school!'

'Hmm,' Honest John said thoughtfully. He picked up the apple and took a bite out of it. 'Then you haven't heard of the easy road to success?'

Pinocchio looked puzzled.

'I'm speaking, my boy, of the theatre!'

16

Honest John went on, drawing his cloak around himself. 'Bright lights! Music! Applause! Fame!'

'Fame?' Pinocchio repeated.

'Yes,' boomed Honest John, turning Pinocchio this way and that. 'He's a natural-born actor, isn't he, Giddy?'

'But I'm going –' Pinocchio began.

'Straight to the top!' Honest John cut in slyly. 'I can see your name in lights! Er – what *is* your name?'

'Pinocchio,' the puppet replied.

'We're wasting precious time!' Honest John walked off, twirling his cane. 'Come, to the theatre!'

Pinocchio hurried after him, and so did Gideon.

'Hi diddle dee dee, an actor's life for me!' sang Honest John loudly. He was thinking about all the money Stromboli would pay him for a real wooden puppet for his show.

Chapter Four

'Fine conscience I turned out to be!' Jiminy Cricket panted. He jammed his hat on his head as he hopped along the street. 'Late the first day! Still, he can't get into much trouble between here and school.'

The cricket looked round as he heard someone singing, 'Hi diddle dee dee, an actor's life for me!'

Honest John, Pinocchio and Gideon marched past, singing loudly. Jiminy's eyes almost popped out of his head.

Jiminy dashed along behind them.

'Pinoke!' he yelled, hopping on to Honest John's tail, climbing up him and scrambling on to his hat.

'Hey, Pinoke!' Jiminy whistled as loudly as he could.

Honest John stopped singing. 'What was that?'

'Oh, it's Jiminy!' Pinocchio cried.

'Huh?' Honest John looked puzzled. 'My boy, you must be seeing things!'

Gideon had spotted Jiminy on his friend's hat. He whipped a mallet out of his coat, and crept up on the cricket. But Jiminy hopped away just as Gideon brought the mallet down on Honest John's hat.

Honest John crumpled to the ground, his hat jammed right down over his head.

'Oh, Jiminy!' Pinocchio said happily. 'I'm going to be an actor!'

'Remember what I said about temptation?' Jiminy said sternly, twirling his umbrella. 'Well, that's him!' He pointed at Honest John.

'Oh no, Jiminy,' Pinocchio said. 'That's Honest John.'

Gideon was trying to pull Honest John's hat off his head, but it was jammed on tightly.

'GET ME OUT OF HERE!' the fox roared furiously.

'All right then,' Jiminy whispered to Pinocchio, 'here's what we'll tell 'em. You can't go to the theatre. You're sorry, but you've got to go to school.'

'Pinocchiooooo!' called Honest John, who'd managed to get the hat off at last. 'Ah, there you are!'

'Here they come, Pinoke,' Jiminy told him. 'Now, you tell 'em.'

'Where were we?' Honest John grinned. 'Ah, yes! On to the theatre!'

'Goodbye, Jiminy!' Pinocchio called, trotting after Honest John.

'Goodbye?' Jiminy gasped. 'Hey, Pinoke – you *can't* go!'

But Pinocchio had already gone, singing, 'Hi diddle dee dee, an actor's life for me!'

'Oh, what'll I do?' Jiminy groaned. 'I'll run and tell his father. No, that'd be snitching. I'll go after him myself!'

Chapter Five

'Ladies and gentlemen!' Stromboli twirled his large black moustache and grinned at the large audience in front of him. 'Stromboli, the master showman, is presenting to you something you will absolutely refuse to believe!'

Jiminy had followed Pinocchio to Stromboli's tent. Now he hopped up on to a nearby lamp to listen. 'Well, it looks like a sell-out!' he muttered, staring at the crowd of people.

'Introducing the only marionette who can sing and dance absolutely without strings!' Stromboli boomed. 'The one and only Pinocchio!'

Jiminy watched as the curtain rose. Puppets playing trumpets appeared, and

21

then a second curtain rose. Pinocchio stood at the top of some stairs and began to sing, 'I got no strings to hold me down, to make me fret or make me frown. I had strings but now I'm free, there are no strings on me!'

The audience began to clap, and Pinocchio beamed. He was starting to enjoy himself. Then he was joined on stage by some other wooden puppets with strings. Pinocchio danced with two little Dutch girls wearing clogs, and some Russian dancers in furry hats who spun round and kicked their legs out very fast. Meanwhile the audience cheered loudly and clapped.

'There are no strings on me!' Pinocchio panted, falling into a heap on the floor, all tangled up with the other puppets, as the song finished.

Jiminy watched in amazement as the crowd jumped to its feet, and began throwing money on to the stage.

'They like him,' Jiminy muttered, feeling quite dazed. 'Maybe I was wrong . . .'

The cricket turned and walked off down

the street. 'I guess he won't need me any more,' Jiminy said sadly to himself. 'What does an actor want with a conscience anyway?'

Chapter Six

It was dark, and rain was falling. A candle was burning in the window of Geppetto's house. Inside, Geppetto, Figaro and Cleo were waiting for Pinocchio to come home.

'What could have happened to him?' Geppetto said anxiously. 'Where could he be?' He reached for his coat. 'I'd better go out again and look for him!'

Meanwhile, Pinocchio was still feeling very pleased with himself. He was sitting on the table in Stromboli's wagon, watching the showman count out a big pile of gold coins. Stromboli could hardly believe how much money he had made that day.

'Bravo, Pinocchio!' he chuckled, moving another stack of coins aside. 'Two hundred. You are sensational! Three hundred!'

Then he spotted a fake coin, and frowned angrily. Then he grinned slyly to himself. 'For you, my little Pinocchio,' he said, giving him the fake coin.

'For me?' Pinocchio gasped. 'Thanks!' He jumped to his feet. 'I'll run right home and tell my father.'

'Home?' Stromboli began to roar with laughter. He took Pinocchio over to a big birdcage in the corner of the wagon, and flung him inside. 'There!' he snarled, snapping on the padlock. 'This will be your home!'

Looking frightened, Pinocchio grabbed the bars.

'Let me out!' he cried.

Stromboli climbed on to the driver's seat and shook the horse's reins. 'Get along there!' he shouted.

The cage swayed as the wagon began to move. Rain was still falling and now thunder was crashing and there were silver flashes of lightning. Pinocchio felt very scared.

'Jiminy!' he called helplessly. Then he

remembered what the cricket had told him, and he began to whistle as loudly as he could. But a loud crash of thunder made Pinocchio jump. He put his hands over his ears, and began to cry.

Jiminy was sitting in the street under his umbrella. He watched Stromboli's wagon go past, and sighed.

'Well, there he goes,' he muttered. 'Sitting in the lap of luxury. I'll just go out of his life quietly . . .'

Sadly Jiminy walked off down the street. But then he stopped.

'Would like to wish him luck, though,' he said to himself.

Jiminy turned and ran after the wagon. Jumping up on to the step, he climbed in.

'Jiminy!' Pinocchio called from the cage. 'Gee, I'm glad to see you!'

'Pinocchio!' Jiminy dashed over to him. 'Now, don't you worry, son. I'll have you out of here in no time!'

Jiminy leaned into the keyhole of the padlock to take a look, and fell inside.

Geppetto painted a smiling face on the wooden puppet.

'A real boy! It's my wish come true!' Geppetto swung
Pinocchio into the air.

'A lie keeps growing and growing until it's as plain as the nose on your face,' said the Blue Fairy.

Pleasure Island sounded like great fun!

'Stuff yourselves! It's all free, boys!' called the man at the gates

'So this is where I find you!' Jiminy said sternly.

Pinocchio felt donkey ears sprout from his head, and then
a tail from the seat of his trousers.

'What a big place!' Pinocchio gurgled.

Deep in the belly of the whale, Geppetto was fishing for food.

The raft shot out of Monstro's mouth, onto the sea.

Pinocchio listened anxiously. He could hear thumps and rattles coming from inside the padlock. Soon Jiminy emerged, looking crestfallen. Pinocchio was trapped.

Chapter Seven

'A fine conscience I turned out to be,' Jiminy said, as Pinocchio began to cry.

'I should have listened to you, Jiminy,' the puppet sobbed. 'I guess I'll never see my father again!'

Jiminy took out his handkerchief to dry Pinocchio's tears. 'Take it easy, son,' he said gently. 'Oh, well, it's stopped raining anyway.'

A bright star was shining in the dark night sky. Jiminy stared up at it.

'Hey!' he yelled excitedly. 'That star again! That lady – the fairy!'

Pinocchio looked scared. 'What'll she say?' he muttered. 'What'll I tell her?'

'You might tell her the truth!' Jiminy said sternly, but Pinocchio bent over and hid his

face in his arms. Feeling rather nervous
himself, Jiminy dived into the seed tray.

The star drifted into the wagon, and
began to spin. Then the sparkling circles
disappeared to reveal the beautiful Blue
Fairy.

'Why, Pinocchio!' the fairy said gently.
'Sir Jiminy!'

Jiminy's head appeared out of a pile of
birdseed. 'This is a pleasant surprise!' he
said nervously.

'Pinocchio, why didn't you go to school?'
the Blue Fairy asked.

'Tell her!' Jiminy said.

'I *was* going to school,' Pinocchio
mumbled, 'till I met somebody.'

'Met somebody?' the fairy said.

'Two big monsters!' Pinocchio replied
quickly. 'With big green eyes!'

Jiminy groaned. But something very
strange was happening to Pinocchio as he
told these fibs. His wooden nose was
beginning to grow. Looking surprised,
Pinocchio put out his hand and felt it.

The fairy raised her eyebrows. 'Monsters? Weren't you afraid?'

'No, ma'am,' Pinocchio boasted. 'But they tied me up in a big sack!'

Pinocchio's nose grew again. This time leaves began to shoot from the tip of it.

'You don't say,' the Blue Fairy gasped. 'And where was Sir Jiminy?'

'They put him in a little sack,' Pinocchio lied.

This time Pinocchio's nose grew so long that it shot out between the bars of the cage.

'How did you escape?' the Blue Fairy went on.

'I didn't,' Pinocchio said. 'They chopped me into firewood!'

A bird's nest appeared on the end of Pinocchio's nose, and two baby birds hatched from the eggs inside.

'Oh! My nose!' Pinocchio gasped. 'What's happened?'

'Perhaps you haven't been telling the truth, Pinocchio,' the Blue Fairy said gently.

'*Perhaps!*' sniffed Jiminy, crossly.

'Oh, but I have,' Pinocchio said. 'Every single word!'

The nest started shaking on the end of his nose, and the birds flew off. Pinocchio looked sadly at the Blue Fairy.

'Please help me,' he cried. 'I'm awful sorry!'

'You see, Pinocchio, a lie keeps growing and growing until it's as plain as the nose on your face,' the Blue Fairy told him.

'You'd better come clean, Pinoke,' Jiminy said.

'I'll never lie again,' Pinocchio promised. 'Honest, I won't!'

'Please, Miss Fairy,' Jiminy added. 'Give him another chance.'

'I'll forgive you this once,' the Blue Fairy agreed. 'But remember, a boy who won't be good might just as well be made of wood!'

'We'll be good,' said Jiminy and Pinocchio together.

'Very well.' The Blue Fairy touched Pinocchio's long nose with her wand.

'But this is the last time I can help you.' And she disappeared.

'Look, my nose!' Pinocchio shouted happily. It was back to normal again.

'Hey, we're free!' Jiminy gasped, pointing at the open padlock. 'Come on, Pinoke!'

They hurried to the back of the wagon and slid out of the door. Not far away in the Red Lobster Inn, Honest John and Gideon were enjoying themselves. They were holding mugs of beer and smoking cigars.

'Hi diddle dee dee, an actor's life for me!' Honest John laughed. 'And the dummy fell for it!' He grinned at the fat man sitting next to him, and dropped a bulging bag of gold coins on to the table. 'And did Stromboli pay! Ha, ha, ha!'

The man, who was dressed in a coachman's uniform, eyed the bag of money. 'How would you blokes like to make some *real* money?'

And he threw a bag of coins down on to the table.

'You see,' he went on in a whisper, 'I'm collecting stupid little boys!'

Honest John looked puzzled. 'Stupid little boys?'

'You know,' the coachman whispered. 'The ones who play hookey from school.' He lowered his voice even more. 'And I takes them to Pleasure Island!'

'Pleasure Island!' Honest John looked very nervous. 'But, the law! Suppose they –?'

'No,' the coachman growled. 'There is no risk. They never come back – as boys!'

His wicked smile frightened even Honest John and Gideon.

'Now, here's where you come in,' the coachman chuckled. 'I've got a coachload leaving at midnight. Any good prospects you find, bring 'em to me!'

Meanwhile, Pinocchio and Jiminy were hurrying along the cobbled street towards Geppetto's house.

'Nothing can stop me now,' Pinocchio was saying firmly. 'I'll make good this time!'

'You'd better!' Jiminy warned him.

'I will,' Pinocchio said. 'I'm going to school! I'd rather be smart than be an actor.'

'Come on,' Jiminy laughed. 'I'll race you home!'

They both ran across the bridge and down the street, but suddenly a cane shot out and hooked Pinocchio. Jiminy didn't see, and carried on running.

'Well, Pinocchio,' said Honest John cheerfully. 'What's your rush?'

'I gotta beat Jiminy home!' Pinocchio panted.

'How's the great actor?' Honest John asked.

'Stromboli was terrible!' Pinocchio told him. 'He locked me in a birdcage! But I learned my lesson –'

'Oh, you poor, poor boy!' Honest John broke in. 'You must be a nervous wreck.' He held Pinocchio's wrist and pretended to take his pulse. 'My, just as I thought!' he groaned. 'A slight touch of monetary complications with bucolic semi-lunar contraptions of the flying trapezius! Close your eyes.'

Honest John whipped out his spotted hanky, and placed it in front of Pinocchio's face. 'Open them. Now what do you see?'

'Spots!' replied Pinocchio.

'Aha!' Honest John said loudly. 'This makes it perfectly clear. My boy, you are allergic!'

'Allergic?' Pinocchio repeated.

'Yes, and there's only one cure,' Honest John went on. 'A vacation on Pleasure Island! That happy land of carefree boys where every day's a holiday!'

'Thanks, but –' Pinocchio began.

'I insist,' Honest John said firmly. 'Come, the coach departs at midnight.'

He and Gideon each took one of Pinocchio's arms and, swinging him between them, they walked off.

Jiminy had noticed, at last, that Pinocchio wasn't with him any more. He was standing on a ledge looking for him and calling his name.

Suddenly, Jiminy heard voices.

'Hi diddle dee dee, it's Pleasure Isle for me!'

Honest John, Gideon and Pinocchio were walking off down the street. Jiminy could hardly believe his eyes. After everything that Pinocchio had said!

Chapter Eight

'Well, here we go again!' Jiminy sighed. He had followed them to the crossroads, and watched Pinocchio climb up on to the seat next to the coachman. Jiminy had managed to hook his umbrella on to the back, before the ugly, grim-faced coachman had driven away. Now he was sitting in the swinging umbrella, wondering what was going to happen next.

Pinocchio was feeling very excited. Pleasure Island sounded like great fun, much better than going to school. And the coach was crammed with real live boys! There was one sitting next to him right now.

'My name's Lampwick,' the boy told Pinocchio, spitting on the floor. 'What's yours?'

'Pinocchio,' the puppet replied.

Lampwick took aim with his slingshot and fired. 'Ever been to Pleasure Island?' he asked. 'They say it's a swell joint. No school, no cops.'

The coachman grinned to himself.

At last the coach reached the harbour, where a large paddle steamer stood waiting for them. Yelling and cheering, Pinocchio, Lampwick and all the other boys dashed out of the coach and on to the boat. Immediately it set sail towards an island in the distance.

When the boat docked, two huge wooden gates swung open. Inside was Pleasure Island, a huge funfair with every kind of ride. There were helter-skelters, big wheels and merry-go-rounds.

'Hurry, hurry, hurry!' called the man at the gates. 'Get your cakes, pies and ice cream here. Eat all you can! Stuff yourselves! It's all free, boys!'

There was a tent called the rough house where some of the boys were fighting, and cigars and tobacco were being given out for free, as well as food.

Jiminy had got lost in the crowds, but now he'd managed to find Pinocchio. He hopped around, trying not to get trodden on.

'Pinocchio!' he yelled. 'There's something phoney about all this!'

But Pinocchio couldn't hear him above the noise of all the boys enjoying themselves.

'I've gotta get him out of here,' Jiminy muttered to himself.

Meanwhile, the coachman was standing on the bridge, giving orders to his men.

'Come on,' he roared. 'Shut the doors and lock 'em tight! Now get below and get them crates ready!'

The coachman glanced at the boys who were still running around enjoying themselves. 'Give a bad boy enough rope, and he'll soon make a jackass of himself!' he muttered, and he chuckled to himself. The big wooden doors swung shut, trapping the boys inside.

*

The Pleasure Island funfair was in ruins. It was dark and silent. All the bright lights had gone out, the rides had stopped and there was no one around. Jiminy picked his way through all the rubbish, trying to find Pinocchio.

Pinocchio was in the pool hall with Lampwick. They were smoking cigars, drinking beer and playing pool.

'Where do you suppose all the kids went, Lampwick?' Pinocchio asked, puzzled.

'Aw, they're around here somewheres,' Lampwick replied, bending over the pool table. 'What do you care? You're having a good time, ain't ya?'

'I sure am!' Pinocchio grinned. But secretly he felt a bit sick from the beer and cigar smoke.

At that moment Jiminy slipped under the pool-hall door.

'Pinocchio!' he yelled, just as Pinocchio made his shot. Pinocchio jumped and fell flat on his face on the pool table.

'So this is where I find you!' Jiminy said

sternly. Dazed, Pinocchio lifted his head to look at him. He still had his cigar in his mouth, although it was rather squashed.

Jiminy sighed. 'How do you ever expect to be a real boy!' he groaned. 'Look at yourself! Smoking! Playing pool!'

'Hey!' Lampwick picked up Jiminy and stared at him. 'Who's the beetle?'

'Let go!' Jiminy shouted angrily, swinging his umbrella at Lampwick.

'He's my conscience,' Pinocchio replied. 'He tells me what's right and wrong.'

Lampwick looked shocked. 'D'you mean to tell me you take orders from a *grasshopper*?'

'Grasshopper!' Jiminy yelled furiously, jumping on to one of the balls on the table. 'Now you listen to me. It wouldn't hurt *you* to take orders from your conscience – if you have one!'

'Yeah, yeah,' Lampwick sneered. He hit the ball Jiminy was standing on and sent it whizzing into the corner pocket. Jiminy went with it.

'Why, you young hoodlum!' Jiminy spluttered, climbing back on to the table. 'I'll knock your block off!'

Lampwick burst out laughing.

'Oh, don't hurt him, Jiminy!' Pinocchio cried. 'He's my best friend!'

Jiminy stared at Pinocchio. 'Your best friend!' he said scornfully, feeling very hurt. 'And what am I? Just your conscience! That settles it!'

And the cricket marched off, leaving Lampwick still laughing.

'Huh! Lampwick!' Jiminy snorted, as he made his way through the funfair. 'After all I tried to do for him! Who's his conscience, anyway? Me or Lampwick? I'm taking the next boat out of here!'

The doors of Pleasure Island were locked. Jiminy rapped on them with his umbrella.

'Open up that door!' he shouted. 'I want to go home!'

A loud noise made Jiminy start. It was the sound of donkeys braying.

'Lively there, now!' roared the coachman. 'We haven't got all night!'

Jiminy peered through a crack in the door. He saw a gang of men loading donkeys into crates and then on to the boat.

'Where do all the donkeys come from?' Jiminy wondered, sliding under the door to get a better look.

One of the men grabbed a donkey and tossed it over to the coachman.

'Come on, let's have another,' the coachman growled. 'What's your name?'

The donkey brayed loudly.

'Okay, you'll do,' the coachman shouted. 'In you go!'

The coachman cracked his whip, and the donkeys shrank back, looking frightened.

'Quiet!' the coachman roared. 'You boys had your fun – now pay for it!'

Jiminy blinked. 'Boys!' he gasped. 'So that's it! Pinocchio!'

And he turned and ran as fast as he could back to the pool hall.

Chapter Nine

'Huh!' Lampwick picked up another glass of beer. 'To hear that beetle talk, you'd think that something was gonna happen to us!'

At that very moment two large, grey, donkey's ears grew out of his head. Pinocchio stared at his friend. Then he looked down at his beer mug and shook his head to clear it.

'Aw, phooey!' Lampwick muttered, as a long, grey tail shot out of the seat of his trousers. 'What's he think I look like? A jackass?'

Lampwick's face turned into a donkey's, and Pinocchio smiled.

'You sure do!' he laughed. The laugh turned into a donkey's bray, and Pinocchio clapped his hand over his mouth.

Lampwick laughed, but then his laugh changed into a bray, too.

'Did that come out of me?' Lampwick spluttered.

Looking very frightened, Pinocchio nodded.

Lampwick felt his cheeks and ears. 'Hey! What's going on?' He ran to a mirror, peered in and gave a yell. 'Help!'

'Maa!' Lampwick brayed. He had turned into a donkey.

Lampwick began kicking out in a fright and Pinocchio backed away. 'Oh, what's happened?' he gasped, feeling donkey ears sprout from his own head, and then a tail from the seat of his trousers.

'Pinocchio!' Jiminy shouted, running towards him.

'Jiminy, help!' Pinocchio wailed.

'Quick, Pinoke!' Jiminy panted. 'They're all donkeys!' He stared at Pinocchio. 'You, too!' he groaned. 'Come on – quick! Before you get any worse!'

Jiminy and Pinocchio ran as fast as they

could. Jiminy had found a way out over the rocks, which led them high up on to a rocky cliff above the sea.

'Hurry up before they see us,' Jiminy told Pinocchio, as they reached the edge of the cliff. 'Ya gotta jump!'

They fell into the water with a SPLASH, and began to swim. At last they reached the shore, soaking wet and shivering.

Pinocchio and Jiminy set off on the long walk back to the village. Pinocchio couldn't wait to see Geppetto again. He was very tired, but when at last they reached the village he began to run towards Geppetto's house.

'Father!' he called. 'I'm home!'

Pinocchio knocked, and then pulled the bell, but nobody came.

'Maybe he's asleep,' Jiminy said, and hopped up on to the ledge to take a look.

But the room was empty. Figaro and Cleo were both gone, too.

'He ain't here,' Jiminy told Pinocchio.

Pinocchio looked frightened. 'Maybe something awful happened to him!'

High above their heads a bright star twinkled in the sky. A white dove flew from the star towards them, and dropped a piece of paper in front of Pinocchio and Jiminy.

'Hey!' said Jiminy, taking out his glasses. 'It's a message about your father!'

'Where is he?' Pinocchio asked eagerly.

Jiminy hopped back and forth, reading the piece of paper. 'It says here that he went looking for you, and he was swallowed by a whale. But he's alive!'

'Alive?' Pinocchio's voice was full of hope. 'Where?'

'Inside a whale called Monstro – at the bottom of the sea!' Jiminy told him.

'Bottom of the sea!' Pinocchio gasped, and immediately he ran off. He had to find his father.

Chapter Ten

Pinocchio stood on a cliff top looking out over the sea. He was tying his tail round a rock as Jiminy rushed up to him.

Pinocchio held out his hand to the cricket. 'Goodbye, Jiminy,' he said.

Jiminy looked surprised. 'I'm with you!' he said, hopping on to the rock and holding his nose. 'Come on!'

Pinocchio jumped into the sea. The rock tied to his tail made him very heavy, and he and Jiminy sank quickly under the water. Down, down, down they dropped, right down to the ocean-bed.

'What a big place!' Pinocchio gurgled, looking at the fish swimming all around them. Pinocchio and Jiminy went on their way, asking the fishes and the clams and the sea horses if they knew where Monstro could be found. But the sea creatures were too scared to tell them.

Monstro was not far away, however. The huge whale was lying on the seabed, and he was fast asleep.

Inside the whale's belly, Geppetto and Figaro were sitting in their boat fishing for food. Cleo was there, too, still in her glass bowl.

'We can't hold out much longer,' Geppetto sighed. 'I never thought it would end this way. Starving to death in the belly of a whale! My poor little Pinocchio . . .'

Monstro had just opened one eye and spotted a school of fish swimming past him. Quickly the whale pretended to be asleep again. Then he spun round and began chasing the fish with his mouth wide open. As he crashed through the water, Pinocchio saw him.

'Monstro!' gasped Pinocchio.

The whale was even bigger than Pinocchio had imagined.

The whale was gobbling everything in front of him. Pinocchio tried to swim up to the surface of the water, but the whale followed him. He opened his mouth wide and swallowed Pinocchio, along with lots more fish.

'Open up, blubbermouth!' called Jiminy, who had been left outside. 'I gotta get in there!'

Meanwhile, Geppetto and Figaro were collecting as many fish as they could. Geppetto cast in his line again and again, tossing the fish over his head on to the deck of the boat. He hooked Pinocchio and reeled him in.

'P–Pinocchio!' Geppetto could hardly believe his eyes as Pinocchio jumped into his arms. 'My boy! I'm so happy to see you!'

Figaro rushed over to say hello, and Cleo bounced up and down happily in her bowl.

'We're all together again!' Geppetto said joyfully. 'You shouldn't have come here! But I'm awfully glad to see you.'

He removed Pinocchio's hat and the donkey ears shot up into view.

'Oh!' Geppetto gasped.

'Oh, that's nothing,' Pinocchio laughed. 'I've got a tail too!'

His laugh turned into a donkey's bray.

'Oh, never mind,' Geppetto said kindly, hugging Pinocchio tightly. 'I've built a raft, but it's hopeless,' he sighed. 'But we can make a nice fire and cook some of the fish.'

Pinocchio suddenly had an idea. 'A great big fire!' he shouted. 'Lots of smoke! Quick, some wood!'

Pinocchio rushed to collect a big pile of wood. Geppetto and Figaro began to help, too. They thought they were going to cook the fish, but Pinocchio was planning something else.

'We're getting out!' Pinocchio told them, grabbing the lantern. He threw it on to the pile of wood, and it started to burn. 'We'll make him sneeze!' Pinocchio said.

Chapter Eleven

Monstro was asleep, floating on top of the water. Smoke drifted out of his spout, and he began to stir. Looking puzzled, he opened his mouth.

'Well, it's about time!' yelled Jiminy, who was sitting on a bottle. He began to paddle forwards into Monstro's mouth.

Meanwhile, Geppetto, Pinocchio, Figaro and Cleo were clinging to the raft, trying to push their way out.

'Hurry, Father!' Pinocchio cried. 'Climb aboard!'

'We'll never get by those teeth,' Geppetto said, looking worried.

'Hey, which way you goin'?' shouted Jiminy, seeing the raft bobbing past him. 'Wait for me!'

Pinocchio and Geppetto paddled hard as they reached the opening.

'Hang on!' called Pinocchio. 'Here we go!'

The raft shot out of Monstro's mouth on to the sea. Jiminy followed them, still clinging to the bottle.

But suddenly the raft began to go backwards, back towards Monstro as the whale took a breath.

'It's no use,' Geppetto groaned, as they were drawn back towards Monstro. 'We're done for!'

But then the whale sneezed. The raft was sent spinning away across the sea again in a whirlpool of waves. Looking furious, the whale charged after the raft, trying to catch up with them. But suddenly he gave up, and sank beneath the waves.

Next moment the raft flew up into the air as Monstro swam underneath it. Everyone was thrown off into the water. Pinocchio quickly climbed back on, and pulled Geppetto on, too.

'He's coming back!' he shouted. 'Hurry!'

Pinocchio and Geppetto began paddling as hard as they could. But Monstro swam after them, and raised his giant tail high above their heads.

'Jump!' yelled Geppetto.

Pinocchio and his father jumped into the water, just as the whale's huge tail smashed the raft into pieces.

'Swim for the shore, Pinocchio!' Geppetto called weakly. He was hanging on to a floating log, looking very tired. Suddenly, the log sank, and Geppetto went with it.

Pinocchio dived underwater and lifted his father back to the surface. Then he swam for the shore, pulling his father with him.

Geppetto and Pinocchio lay on the sand, worn out. Figaro was washed up beside them, clinging to a wooden board. Then Cleo arrived, still in her fishbowl. At last, Jiminy was thrown up on to the sand, too.

'Pinocchio!' Jiminy gasped. His friend was lying face down on the shore. He wasn't moving at all . . .

❄

'My boy,' sighed Geppetto, sadly. He had carried Pinocchio home and laid him gently on the bed. 'My brave little boy.'

Jiminy took out his hanky and wiped his eyes. Figaro and Cleo were crying, too. They didn't see a bright light drift into the room.

'Prove yourself brave, truthful and unselfish, and some day you will be a real boy!' said the Blue Fairy's voice softly.

The light grew brighter.

'Awake, Pinocchio, awake!' the Blue Fairy said.

The light disappeared. Pinocchio sat up and rubbed his eyes. His donkey ears and tail had gone. And he wasn't wooden anymore. He was a real boy!

'Father!' Pinocchio called. 'What're you crying for?'

'Because you're dead, Pinocchio,' Geppetto sobbed.

'No, I'm not!' Pinocchio laughed. 'I'm alive! And I'm real!'

Geppetto rushed over to take a look. 'You *are* a real boy!' he gasped as Jiminy, Figaro and Cleo smiled happily. 'This calls for a celebration!'

Geppetto wound up the musical boxes, and he, Pinocchio and Figaro began to dance around the room.

'Well, this is where I came in!' Jiminy smiled to himself. He looked out of the window at a very bright star high up in the sky. 'Thank you,' he said softly. 'He deserved to be a real boy!'

A twinkling light touched Jiminy's coat. The cricket looked down, and there was a gold badge. It said *Official Conscience*.

'My!' Jiminy beamed. 'Solid gold, too!' He stared up at the star. 'When you wish upon a star, your dreams come true . . .'